Surfing and Other EXTREME WATER SPORTS

by Drew Lyon

CAPSTONE PRESS
a capstone imprint

Edge Books is published by Capstone Press,
an imprint of Capstone.
1710 Roe Crest Drive
North Mankato, Minnesota 56003
www.capstonepub.com

Library of Congress Cataloging-in-Publication Data
is available on the Library of Congress website.
ISBN: 978-1-5435-9005-0 (hardcover)
ISBN: 978-1-4966-6610-9 (paperback)
ISBN: 978-1-5435-9009-8 (ebook pdf)

Editorial Credits
Anna Butzer, editor; Cynthia Della-Rovere, designer;
Kelly Garvin, media researcher; Katy LaVigne,
production specialist

Photo Credits
Alamy: Allan Seiden/Pacific Stock/Design Pics Inc, 22, Stephen Frink Collection, 10; Associated Press/Hugo
Silva/Red Bull Content Pool, 5; Getty Images: Craig Pulsifer, 16, Stefan Matzke-sampics/Corbis, 7; iStockphoto/
Richinpit, cover, back cover; Newscom/DENIS BALIBOUSE/REUTERS, 24; Shutterstock: Anna Moskvina, 14,
C Levers, 12 (top), EpicStockMedia, 9, 19, Jeff Whyte, 27, Konstantin Faraktinov, 12 (middle right), Roberto
Caucino, 29, Sing5pan, 12 (bottom), Vaclav Mach, 12 (middle left), wavebreakmedia, 13, Yulia Melnikova, 21

Artistic elements: Shutterstock: pupsy, Ryan Janssens, Willyam Bradberry

All internet sites appearing in back matter were available and accurate when this book was sent to press.

Table of Contents

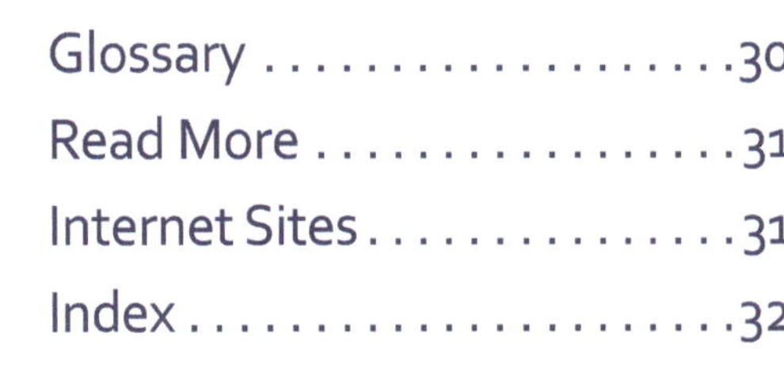

Sweet Dreams

Sometimes, when it's least expected, dreams come true. In 2017, pro surfer Rodrigo Koxa rode the wave of a lifetime in Nazaré, Portugal. On the eve of a competition at Nazaré Beach, Koxa's dream brought visions of a huge wave.

"I had an amazing dream the night before, where I was talking to myself: 'You gotta go straight down. You gotta go straight down,'" said Koxa, who started surfing at the age of five. "I didn't really know what it meant. But I figured somebody was talking to me. ... It was amazing."

Rodrigo Koxa (right) surfs a big wave in Nazaré, Portugal in 2017.

Koxa's dream became reality at Nazaré when he set the world record for the largest wave ever surfed. The massive wave measured 80 feet (24 meters) high, 2 feet (61 centimeters) higher than the previous record. A wave this epic only comes around once—if you're lucky. It took less than a minute for Koxa to complete the ride.

But Koxa's moment in the sun almost never happened. Several years before his record-setting triumph, a **gnarly** wave in Nazaré nearly killed Koxa. His confidence was crushed. The close call led to nightmares and Post-Traumatic Stress Disorder (PTSD). Koxa lost the courage and desire to surf.

After a year, Koxa overcame his fears with support from friends and family. When he returned to the ocean, Koxa shied away from big **swells**. He started small before attempting to ride the bigger waves.

Koxa's historic wave in Portugal wasn't the first record-setter of his career. In 2010, he surfed the largest wave recorded in South America, a 60-foot (18-m) swell.

By 2018, Koxa was on top of the surfing world. The stunning video capturing his record ride quickly spread on social media. Setting a world record, Koxa later said, was the best day of his life.

"(The record) makes me feel proud and humble all at once," he said. When a chance at history came his way, Rodrigo Koxa was ready. After all, he'd already dreamed it.

CHAPTER 2

What is Surfing?

More than 70 percent of Earth's surface is water. Many daredevil athletes leave the safety of land sports for natural thrills on water. Some water sports—such as surfing—don't require fancy gear or gadgets. A decent board and big waves are all surfers need for a successful day on the water.

Surfing was invented by Polynesians. Samoans surfed on wooden planks thousands of years ago. European explorers witnessed surfing as early as the 1700s. Over its development, surfing exploded into a worldwide hobby. Surfing grew popular in California during the 1960s. From the Pacific Ocean, surfing culture spread across America and the world.

In surfing, the waves call the shots. A wave is a coach, teammate, and referee. It's never the opponent. Surfers ride with a wave, not against it. But surfers don't follow a scoreboard. They don't watch a clock either. Time seems to stop on a surfboard.

Athletes who don't live near oceans can practice in artificial wave pools.

Ocean coastlines are usually the best surfing spots because the swells are the biggest. But surfers don't have to live near the ocean to **shred** a wave. Technology makes it possible to create "artificial waves" in pools far away from coastal areas.

There are also brave surfers in the Midwest who surf in the frigid waters of the **Great Lakes**, even in winter. Brr! Fortunately, surfers can endure cold waters by wearing **wet suits**. Hardcore surfers debate where the best waves can be found. Some say they're in California, Hawaii, or Australia.

shred—surfing the waves in a successful fashion
Great Lakes—a chain of five large lakes in North America and Canada
wet suit—a close-fitting suit made of material that keeps athletes warm in cold water

Visual Glossary

wax
Surfers rub wax onto their boards. The wax helps them grip the board with their feet while they're riding waves.

earplugs
Surfers in cold water use earplugs to prevent Surfer's Ear, a condition that causes bone growth in ears.

sunscreen
Sufers should always apply sunscreen before going outdoors. Sunscreen helps protect the skin from sun damage.

dry bag
A dry bag is an essential piece of gear for surfers. It's used to store wet towels and suits.

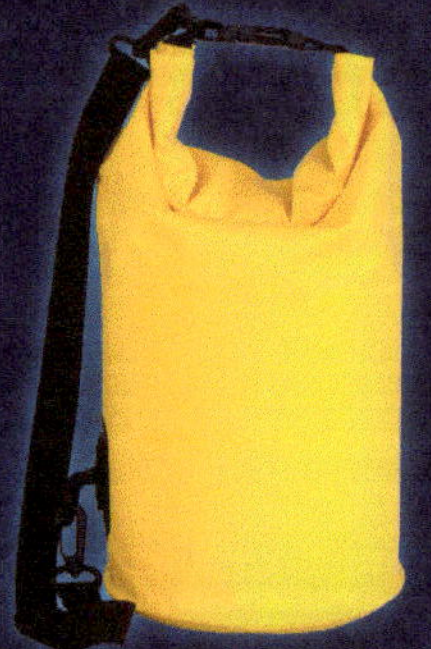

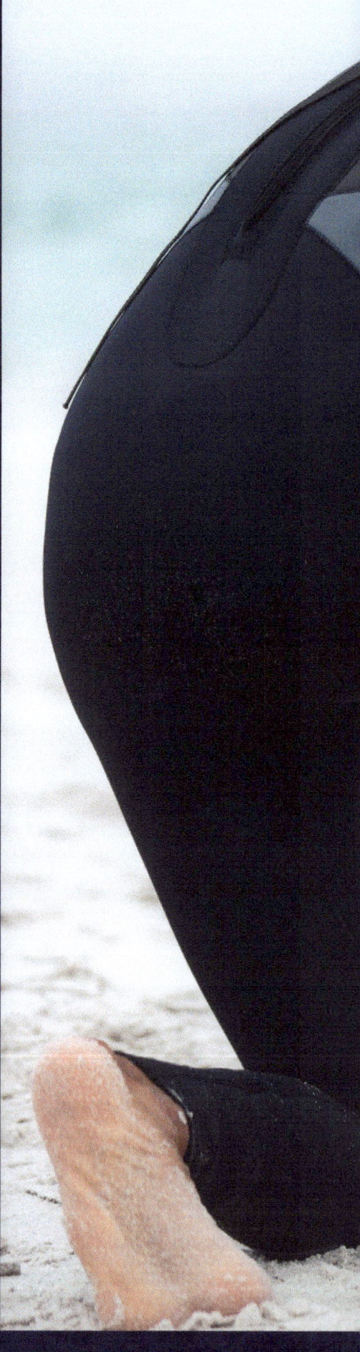

board
The size of a surfboard depends on the individual surfer's height, weight, and experience level. In general, a beginner's surfboard should be about 3 feet (91 centimeters) taller than the surfer.

fins
Surf fins attached to the bottom of a surfboard provide stability and improve performance. There are multiple options for fins: single-fin, twin-fin, thruster, quad, and five-fin setups.

wet suit
Without the comforts of a wet suit, many surfers simply couldn't stay in the water very long.

leash
In case of a fall or accident, a leash connected to the surfer's ankle ensures a board doesn't float away from its owner.

CHAPTER 3

Wakeboarding

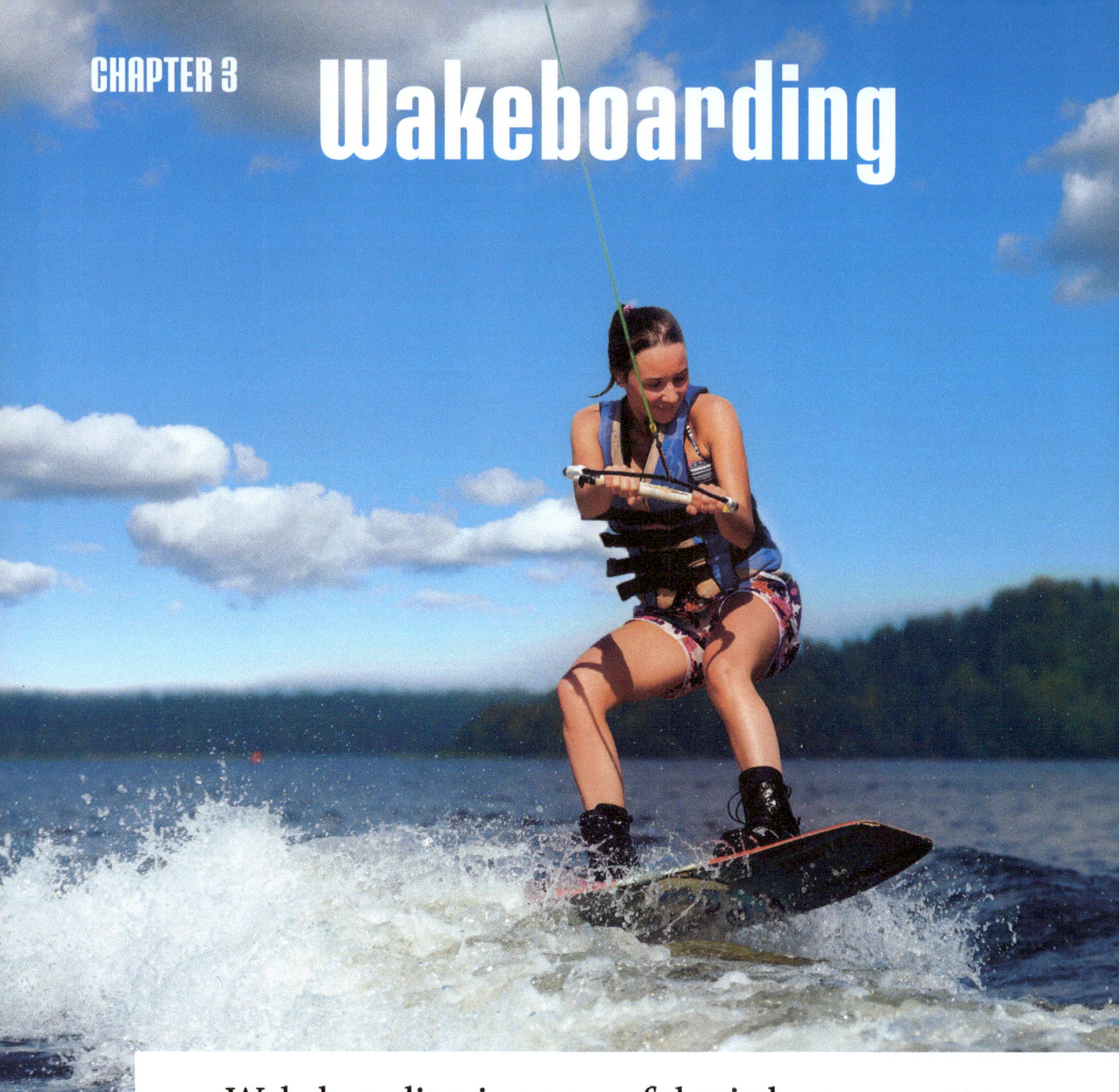

Wakeboarding is a powerful mix between water skiing, surfing, and skateboarding. Wakeboarding is most similar to waterskiing. It involves being pulled by a **motorboat** to travel over the water. However, instead of skis, this sport uses one wide board. A wakeboarder holds on to a rope attached to a boat. As the boat moves, the athlete uses its **wake** for extreme boarding.

Wakeboarding requires flexibility and strength. The best wakeboarders take it to the extreme by performing daring tricks. Some tricks include 360-degree spins, front and back flips, and back rolls. More advanced wakeboarders learn to jump across the length of the wake. But tricks are difficult and should only be tried by experienced boarders. Casual wakeboarders simply enjoy **carving** the wake in the same way a surfer rides a wave.

Every year more than 4 million people strap on to a board, grab a rope, and glide across water.

motorboat—a fast, medium-sized boat that is moved by a motor
wake—the V-shaped trail of waves left behind a moving boat
carve—to make sharp turns on a wake or wave; can be used to describe surfing or wakeboarding

Wakeboarding began as a combination of surfing and waterskiing. While the board might look a little bit like a surfboard, a wakeboard does not require big waves. It just needs the wake created by the boat.

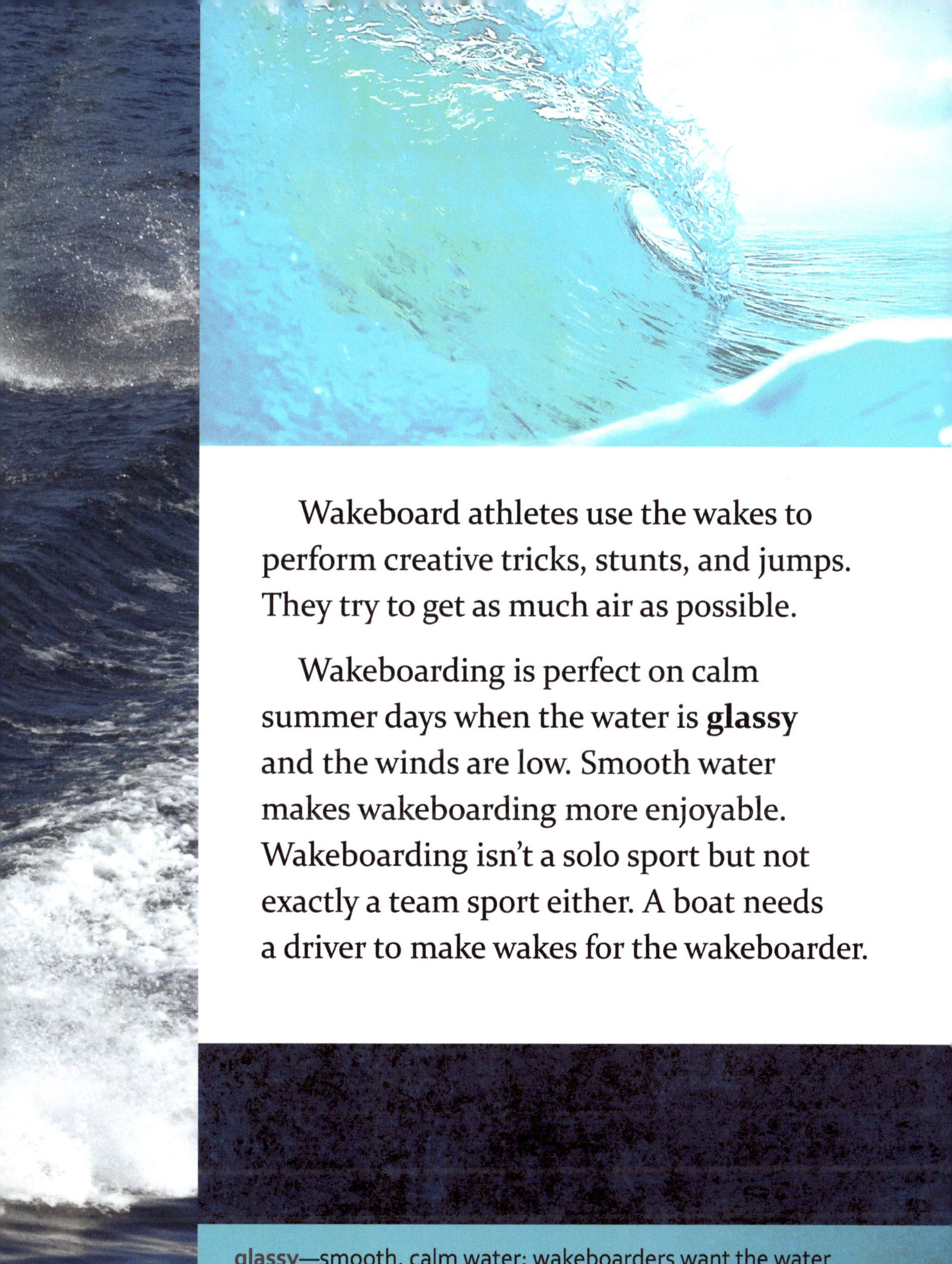

Wakeboard athletes use the wakes to perform creative tricks, stunts, and jumps. They try to get as much air as possible.

Wakeboarding is perfect on calm summer days when the water is **glassy** and the winds are low. Smooth water makes wakeboarding more enjoyable. Wakeboarding isn't a solo sport but not exactly a team sport either. A boat needs a driver to make wakes for the wakeboarder.

glassy—smooth, calm water; wakeboarders want the water to be as glassy as possible

CHAPTER 4

Windsurfing

In some water sports. like wakeboarding, the wind is no friend to an athlete. Windsurfers have the opposite attitude. Windsurfers rely on steady winds for their natural thrills. The ideal wind speeds for windsurfing range from about 10 knots for beginners up to 20 to 30 knots for advanced windsurfers.

Windsurfing combines parts of surfing and sailing. People first began windsurfing in the late 1950s. By the 1970s, it had become popular in North America and Europe. People wanted to show off their skills and find out who was the best. The first world championships were held in 1973. Today windsurfing is an event in the Olympic Games.

Freestyle sailors try to perform the most daring tricks. They ride huge waves and get big air when they do jumps. Racing sailors use wind power to reach top speeds. **Slalom** windsurfing is similar to racing, but it also involves skillfully moving around **obstacles**.

slalom—to move or race in a winding path, avoiding obstacles
obstacle—an object or barrier that competitors must avoid during a race

Windsurfing became a popular extreme water sport with numerous categories: slalom, big air, speed sailing, freestyle, and more.

Windsurfing attracts water sport athletes, from the casual to fanatical. Water sport athletes of all ages windsurf. Children as young as five years old can start windsurfing by using lightweight **sailboards**. Teenagers have even won world windsurfing championships.

sailboard—a wind-powered surf board with a sail mounted on a joint

A breezy day can cause headaches for some water sport athletes. For windsurfers, when the winds pick up, it's time to get out on the water.

CHAPTER 5

Cliff Diving

Surfing, wakeboarding, and windsurfing are popular, but cliff diving is one of the original extreme water sports. Cliff diving began in Hawaii in the 1700s. Hawaiians call cliff diving *lele kawa*, which means "entry with no splash." Cannonballing in cliff diving is a recipe for disaster. The best cliff dives leave hardly any splash. To this day, Native Hawaiians continue honoring their cliff diving history.

A man cliff dives from the Waimea Falls in Oahu, Hawaii.

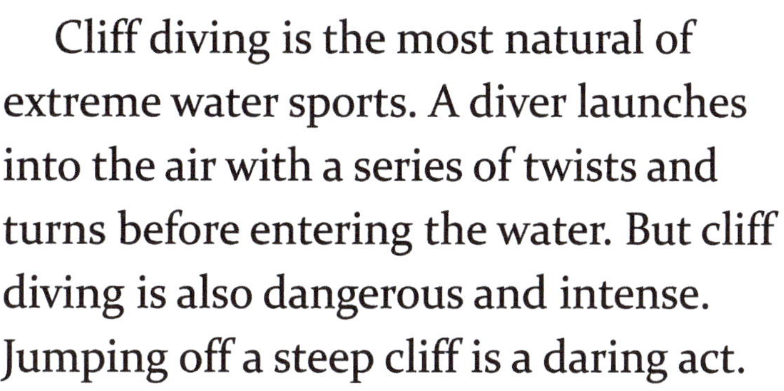

Cliff diving is the most natural of extreme water sports. A diver launches into the air with a series of twists and turns before entering the water. But cliff diving is also dangerous and intense. Jumping off a steep cliff is a daring act.

Cliffs are near bodies of fresh and salt water. Most divers have experience high diving into pools. The only gear a cliff diver needs is a bathing suit. Even jumping into the water in a **pencil dive** brings risks. That's why most cliff divers never dive alone. They use the **buddy system**. The World High Diving Federation says dives higher than 65.5 feet (20 m) should have rescue divers nearby.

pencil dive—a feet-first dive in which the diver makes the body as straight as a pencil
buddy system—pairing up with a partner to ensure each other's safety

A cliff diving athlete jumps from a 69-foot (21-m) high platform during the Red Bull Cliff Diving World Series in Switzerland in 2018.

The Red Bull Cliff Diving World Series has raised the sport's profile. The diving series changes locations featuring lakes, oceans, quarries, cities, and historical landmarks. In 2019, a Cliff Diving World Series event was held in Raouché, Lebanon. Athletes dove off the Pigeon Rocks, which are ancient limestone rocks 88 feet (27 m) above the sea.

At heights up to 92 feet (28 m), World Series divers travel at speeds of roughly 53 miles per hour (85 kilometers per hour). The divers stay in the air for about three seconds before hitting water. When landing, a diver's impact with the water's surface resembles a bomb exploding. Divers learn to spread their arms once entering the water. This helps decrease their speed and keeps them from traveling too deep into the water.

CHAPTER 6

How to Get Started

Water sport athletes should be good swimmers. Anyone who wants to become a water sport athlete should master swimming lessons. Young athletes should always have an adult with them when they are near or in water. All athletes, new or experienced, should wear the proper safety gear.

Water sport athletes constantly risk injury. Bodies of water react to weather in mysterious ways. Lakes and oceans are more dangerous than a pool or playground. Swimmers learn to respect the ocean's power and never let their guards down. Being aware of one's surroundings is key to survival.

A beginner must first get comfortable standing on a surfboard. Before learning to ride a wave, surfers should first learn to stay balanced on a surfboard. This is best achieved by practicing surfer stance on land. Every surfer should start by riding small waves that are just a few feet (1 m) high.

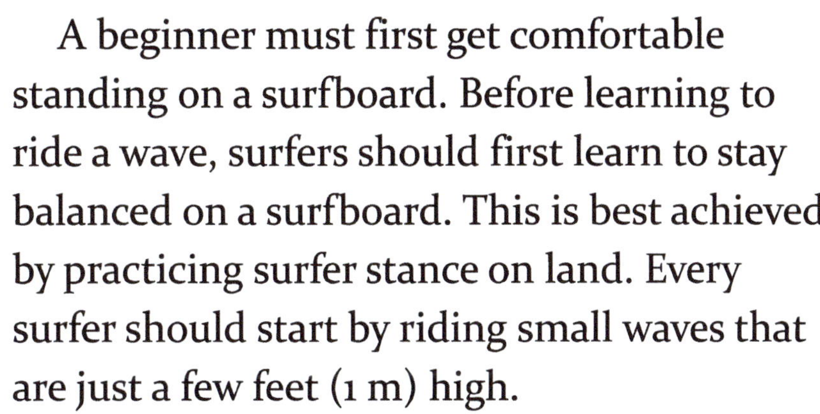

Beginner surfers practice a surfer stance on land before getting in the water.

Similar to surfing, windsurfing beginners should focus on learning to stay balanced on a board. Beginners can start with a large board with a small triangular sail. Sailing on lakes with low wind speeds is the best way for beginner windsurfers to learn.

Keep it simple, take it slow, and always look out in front of you. Distraction is a recipe for a face-first **wipeout**. But don't be afraid to fall—everyone does!

There is a lot to look at out on the water, but it is important to stay focused.

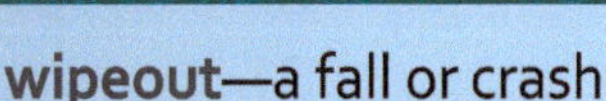

wipeout—a fall or crash

Glossary

buddy system (BUHD-ee SISS-tuhm)—pairing up with a partner to ensure each other's safety

carve (KAHRV)—to make sharp turns on a on a wake or wave; can be used to describe surfing or wakeboarding

glassy (GLA-see)—smooth, calm water; wakeboarders want the water to be as glassy as possible

gnarly (NAAR-lee)—large, nasty

Great Lakes (GRAYT LAKES)—a chain of five large lakes in North America and Canada

motorboat (MOH-tur-bote)—a fast, medium-sized boat that is moved by a motor

obstacle (OB-stuh-kuhl)—an object or barrier that competitors must avoid during a race

pencil dive (PEN-suhl DYV)—a feet-first dive in which the diver makes the body as straight as a pencil

sailboard (SAYL-bord)—a wind-powered surf board with a sail mounted on a joint

shred (SHRED)—surfing the waves in a successful fashion

slalom (SLAH-luhm)—to move or race in a winding path, avoiding obstacles

swell (SWEL)—a large wave with a long, continuous crest

wake (WAYK)—the V-shaped trail of waves left behind a moving boat

wet suit (WET SOOT)—a close-fitting suit made of material that keeps athletes warm in cold water

wipeout (WIPE-out)—a fall or crash

READ MORE

Hamilton, S.L. *Wakeboarding*. Minneapolis: Abdo Publishing, 2016.

Kreie, Chris. *Don't Wobble on the Wakeboard*. North Mankato, MN: Stone Arch Books, 2014.

Loh-Hagan, Virginia. *Extreme Cliff Diving*. Ann Arbor, MI: Cherry Lake Publishing, 2017.

INTERNET SITES

Red Bull: Cliff Diving
www.cliffdiving.redbull.com

Surfer Today: What Is Surfing?
https://www.surfertoday.com/surfing/what-is-surfing

WikiKidz: Wakeboarding
https://wiki.kidzsearch.com/wiki/Wakeboarding

INDEX